visit us at www.abdopublishing.com

Reinforced library bound edition published in 2013 by Spotlight, a division of the ABDO Group, PO Box 398166, Minneapolis, MN 55439. Spotlight produces high-quality reinforced library bound editions for schools and libraries. Published by agreement with Warner Bros.-A Time Warner Company.

Printed in the United States of America, North Mankato, Minnesota.
102012
012013
♻ This book contains at least 10% recycled materials.

Library of Congress Cataloging-in-Publication Data

Kupperberg, Paul.
 Scooby-Doo and the night of the undead! / script, Paul Kupperberg ; artist, Scott Jeralds. -- Reinforced library bound edition.
     pages cm. -- (Scooby-Doo graphic novels)
 ISBN 978-1-61479-050-1
 1. Graphic novels. I. Jeralds, Scott, illustrator. II. Scooby-Doo (Television program) III. Title. IV. Title: Night of the undead!
 PZ7.7.K87Sch 2013
 741.5'973--dc23
                         2012033323

All Spotlight books are reinforced library bindings
and manufactured in the United States of America.

SCOOBY-DOO!

Table of Contents

...IT *ISN'T* HUMAN...AT LEAST NOT ANYMORE! ME AND *JACK* ARE *BIOLOGY STUDENTS* AT THE UNIVERSITY. RECENTLY, WE DISCOVERED A *NEW VIRUS*, RELATED TO *E COLI*, OR THE *FLESH-EATING DISEASE!*

THE VIRUS WAS ISOLATED TO *LAB RATS*... BUT WE STARTED HEARING REPORTS ABOUT *PEOPLE* BEING *INFECTED!*

AND IT'S JUST A *COINCIDENCE* YOU WERE IN THE PARKING LOT WITH A *VIDEO CAMERA* WHEN THIS HAPPENED?!

THE NIGHT OF THE UNDEAD!

SCRIPT: PAUL KUPPERBERG:
ARTIST: SCOTT JERALDS
LETTERING: TRAVIS LANHAM
COLORING: HEROIC AGE
EDITOR: HARVEY RICHARDS
COVER: VINCENT DEPORTER

YEAH, WHAT ARE THE *ODDS*, RIGHT?! WE'D JUST BOUGHT THE CAMERA AT THE MALL AND WERE TESTING IT OUT!

THIS IS *SERIOUS*, YOU GUYS! THIS VIRUS IS *SUPER-CONTAGIOUS*...

SHORTLY...

SO WHAT *ELSE* CAN YOU TELL US ABOUT VIRUS-Z, MAX?

WE KNOW IT'S PASSED BY THE *BITE* OF AN INFECTED PERSON!

ACCORDING TO THE WITNESSES, ONCE A PERSON'S BEEN BITTEN, THEY START TO *CHANGE* ALMOST IMMEDIATELY!

THE LAST SAMPLE WE HAVE OF THE VIRUS IS *DAYS* OLD...

...BUT CONSIDERING HOW FAST IT *MUTATES*, I SURE WOULD LIKE TO GET MY HANDS ON A MORE *RECENT* ONE!

UH...BE... BE *CAREFUL* WHAT YOU *WISH* FOR, MAX...

...LOOK!

WOW! ARE YOU *GETTING* THIS, JACK--?!

I'D LIKE TO GET A *CLOSER* LOOK AT THIS *CREATURE* MYSELF...!

SOON...

FRIENDS OF OURS OWN THIS *VIDEO EDITING STUDIO.* IT'LL JUST TAKE A MINUTE TO SET THINGS UP...!

IT'S *STRANGE* HOW *FEW* ZOMBIES THERE ARE...!

IF THE VIRUS IS *SO CONTAGIOUS* AND THE EFFECT SO *FAST...*

...HOW COME THERE AREN'T *HUNDREDS* OF THEM BY NOW?!

SURE! AS A JOKE, SOME MATHEMATICIANS FIGURED IT WOULD TAKE ZOMBIES, IF THEY EXISTED, JUST *WEEKS* TO INFECT THE *ENTIRE* WORLD!

OKAY! WE'RE READY TO *ROLL!*

THERE'S A *LOT* OF VIDEO TO COVER...!

AND WHILE YOU'RE DOING THAT, *I'LL* BE MAKING A COUPLE OF *PHONE CALLS...!*

WE WANT TO SEE IT *ALL,* MAX...!

HMMM!

NOPE! BECAUSE THERE ARE *NO* ZOMBIES, *ARE* THERE, BOYS?

YOU... YOU *SAW* THEM WITH YOUR OWN EYES!

AND I HAVE, ER... *PROOF...* ON *TAPE...!*

SO DO *WE,* MAX! SUCH AS, *ALL* THE ZOMBIES ON THEM ARE WEARING THE *SAME DOG TAGS* AS YOU AND JACK!

OH, NO! OUR *FRATERNITY TAGS...* THE GUYS *FORGOT* TO TAKE THEM OFF!

MAN! AND WE WERE SO *CAREFUL* TO MAKE THIS AS *REALISTIC* AS POSSIBLE!

WAITAMINNIT! WHAT JUST, LIKE, *HAPPENED--?*

I *CHECKED,* SHAGGY! MAX AND JACK *AREN'T* BIOLOGISTS...

...THEY'RE *FILM STUDENTS!* WE HAVEN'T *REALLY* BEEN CHASING *FLESH-EATING CREATURES--*

--JUST *UNKNOWINGLY* PLAYING *PARTS* IN THE *MOVIE* THEY'RE MAKING WITH THEIR FRIENDS!

AND WE *WOULD* HAVE MADE IT, TOO... IF NOT FOR YOU DUDES!

I'M, LIKE, *SORRY* WE SOLVED THE CASE, GANG! I THINK I WOULD'VE LIKED TO *SEE* THIS MOVIE...!

THE END!

OOOOHHHH...

IT'S COME BACK FOR *ME!*

ROINKS!

YOU'VE GOT *SWAMP MUCK* ON YOUR HEAD...

THAT THING *ATTACKED* ME AND RAN BACK INTO THA BAYOU!

HMMM...

SAMUEL?! ARE YOU ALL RIGHT?

WHEN THA *HURRICANE* CAME UP FROM THE *SOUTH,* IT MISSED MAH RESTAURANT BY NOT MORE THAN 20 FEET.

SAMUEL AND AH COULDN'T BELIEVE OUR *LUCK!* THEN THAT *CREATURE* CAME OUTTA THA BAYOU TO THE *NORTH* AND DESTROYED EVERYTHING AH OWNED!

FROM THE NORTH... THAT'S INTERESTING! I'VE GOT A *HUNCH!*

NOT SO FAST, VELMA. THAT SWAMP'S A *MIGHTY* DANGEROUS PLACE! YOU SHOULD TAKE AN EXPERIENCED GUIDE.

I'LL GO WITH THEM. DON'T YOU WORRY *NONE,* GARY!

ALL RIGHT, BUT DON'T GO DOIN' ANYTHING *STUPID* NOW, YA HEAR?

SURE WON'T. *FOLLOW* ME, GUYS!

DON'T WORRY, WE'RE RIGHT *BEHIND* YOU.

⁂GULP!⁂ YEAH, RIGHT BEHIND YOU.

RE ROO...